The Legend of Big Red

JAMES ROY was born in western New South Wales and spent much of his early life as a missionary child in Papua New Guinea and Fiji. It was here that his love of stories and books began to flourish, and this led to an interest in writing. His second novel, *Full Moon Racing* was a Children's Book Council of Australia Notable Book, received a commendation for the IBBY Ena Noel Award, and was also shortlisted for the Royal Blind Society Talking Book of the Year Awards. *Captain Mack* won Honour Book in the 2000 CBCA Book of the Year Awards: Younger Readers and *A Boat for Bridget* met with critical acclaim and was a CBCA Notable Book. James lives with his family in the Blue Mountains, and enjoys sailing, bushwalking and performing with his band Cranky Franky.

Other books by James Roy

Young Adult Fiction

Almost Wednesday
Full Moon Racing

Younger Readers

Captain Mack
Billy Mack's War
A Boat for Bridget

Steampunk Series

Ichabod Hart and the Lighthouse Mystery

The Legend of Big Red

James Roy
Illustrated by Rae Dale

University of Queensland Press

First published 2005 by University of Queensland Press
Box 6042, St Lucia, Queensland 4067 Australia

Reprinted 2005

www.uqp.uq.edu.au

Typeset by Peripheral Vision
Set in 13/18.6pt Sabon
Printed in Australia by McPherson's Printing Group

Distributed in the USA and Canada by
International Specialized Books Services, Inc.,
5824 N.E. Hassalo Street, Portland, Oregon 97213-3640

Cataloguing–in–Publication Data
National Library of Australia
Roy, James, 1968- .
  The legend of big red.

  Young readers, 9-13 years.

  1. Adventure - Juvenile fiction. I. Title.

A823.3

ISBN 0 7022 3528 8.

For Kyle, formerly of Kariong.

Chapter 1

I can't remember where Barney and I first heard about Big Red. It was just one of those things that the kids of Hunter's Gully talk about at school, or down at the skate ramp or outside Pompelmo's Take-away. But one thing was for sure — while everyone in the local area knew about it, no one could ever say they'd definitely seen it.

Big Red was a fish, an enormous cod. If it did exist, it lived in Bailey's Swamp, which is, in fact, a section of the river that was dammed years ago to make a kind of long, snaking lake in the gully. It was probably given the grand title of 'swamp' when the river had risen only a few metres and was little more than a wide, marshy collection of muddy water. Maybe that's what happens when people get a bit over-excited and name things before they really know what they're talking about. These days, Bailey's Swamp is wide and deep, and the water's clean. It's a great place to muck about fishing, swimming, or paddling around on homemade rafts, and Barney and I have been going there for years. Sometimes we camp, or catch yabbies, sometimes we spot a platypus, often we just swim or drop from the rope-swing my older brother and his mates hung from the big angophora tree years ago.

It's as if Big Red's legend has grown over the years, a bit like the Loch Ness monster. It got its name because of its colour, of course, although Dad says that the legend probably started when some drunk fisherman pulled out an old Heinz tomato soup can and decided to tell his mates that he'd actually hooked a giant cod.

People around here have been talking about Big Red for as long as I can remember. Pretty much every boy and most of the girls in the local area have at some time gone down to the weir to throw in a line, but of course no one's ever caught the big fella. Sure, people talk about nibbles and broken hooks and the water stirring at dusk, and one time a man with a shiny silver four-wheel-drive and a bad bushman's hat was flashing a photo around at the pub. It showed a kind of wet orangey fishy shape, but it just looked to me like a dodgy photo of a goldfish, taken from too close up.

There are parts of Bailey's Swamp you can't walk to, way upriver. I mean, you could if you were really determined, but it would mean climbing around cliffs and through spiky scrub, and it's never seemed like a very appealing idea, especially when you're carrying camping and fishing gear and other stuff.

Then Barney's big brother Tom went and bought a new canoe. It was made of carbon-monoxide fibre or some other hi-tech stuff, and was heaps lighter than his old fibreglass one, which he said Barney could have. Not that Barney and I minded at all that it was old. It was a canoe, and that's all that mattered, and it kept more water out than in. So Barney said thanks straightaway, before Tom had a chance to change his mind.

Suddenly, going upriver became an exciting idea. Imagine that — packing our gear into a boat and heading off to explore the uncharted reaches of the Swamp! It was me who suggested it, and Barney grinned widely and said, 'That's a mad idea! We can make maps and everything, and find a secret harbour, like in that book!'

He was right — it was a mad idea, and by that I mean good-mad, not crazy-mad. The way we saw it, there was only one major

problem: my mum. We knew that Barney's mum wouldn't mind at all, so we decided to ask her first. Then we could go to my mum and say that Mrs Phillmore had already said it was okay. It's a bit unfair on my mum, I know, but when there's a waterway to explore, you need to use whatever methods are going to work. Just imagine if Captain Cook's mum had said he couldn't go exploring. 'It's far too dangerous, James. Who knows what you might run into?'

So we asked Barney's mum, and just like we'd expected, she said, 'Sure, so long as it's okay with Liam's mother.' We went to my place then, and after I'd got Mum a cup of tea and a biscuit, we asked her.

'Where? The Swamp?' she asked, before sipping her tea thoughtfully. 'How long for?'

This was promising. At least she hadn't said no, yet.

'Two nights, that's all,' I said.

'Two nights,' she repeated slowly. 'And

was it going to be just the two of you?'

Not so good. In my head I quickly ran through the list of slightly older kids we could invite along, if that would make the difference between going and not going.

'Because I don't want you taking any girls up there or anything,' Mum continued.

Barney choked on his Milo.

'Girls?' I said. 'Mum, we're twelve!'

'Of course you are,' Mum replied. 'All right then, I guess you're old enough to be sensible.'

'Really?' said Barney. I frowned at him. He wasn't meant to sound so surprised.

'Yes, really,' Mum said. 'But only for one night.'

'But Mum!'

'And you'll take your father's UHF as well. For emergencies, you see. Think of it as a sextant.'

Barney and I looked at each other. Going for one night was definitely better than not going at all.

'Thanks, Mum,' I said. 'Can we take Otto?' The dog heard his name, and he wagged his tail until it became a crazed blur.

'Of course you can take Otto — he'd love it.'

'Awesome! Come on, Barney, time to prepare an Expedition Inventory,' I said.

'A what?'

'A list.'

'Oh.'

Chapter 2

Expedition Inventory for *HMAS* Stoutheart (for reconnoitre of Black Swamp)

Tent (the little red one)

Groundsheet (in case of tent lost overboard, and the onset of ~~inclement~~ ~~encliment~~ bad weather. Also to wrap bodies in before committing to the deep)

Rope — 2 lengths for securing groundsheet (also for keelhauling unruly crew and for securing harpoon to bow of vessel for Nantucket

sleigh-ride)

Harpoon (to be fashioned from star-picket)

Fishing gear

Bait (worms, bread, old prawns. Consider using bits of dead crew if necessary)

Hunting knife

Sextant

Spare batteries for sextant

Map-making stuff (exercise book, pencils)

Compass (magnetic kind, not the kind you draw circles with, Barney)

Sleeping bags

Clothes

Billy and saucepan and knives and forks and bowls. And cups.

Food (decide on the day, but shouldn't rule out eating each other, after drawing lots to decide)

Lots, for drawing (not sure what these are, but shall be acquired)

Coke

Chips

First aid stuff (Barney's mum to get)

Water (if sufficient room in hold of vessel)

Chapter 3

'Is that it?' I said, as we read through the list. 'It doesn't look like much.'

'We don't really want all that much,' Barney replied. 'It's all got to fit in the vessel. Besides, it's only one night,' he added, looking a bit disappointed. He read over the list once more. 'What *is* a Nantucket sleigh-ride, anyway?' he asked.

'I think that's what they called it when olden-day whalers got towed along by a whale, just after they'd harpooned it,' I said.

'Weird name. Sounds like mad fun, though!'

'Okay, focus,' I said. 'Anything we've forgotten?'

'Matches and a torch.'

'Yep, good thinking,' I agreed, adding them to the list. 'Anything else?'

'No, I think that's about it,' said Barney.

'Good. I'll write out a copy for you, but you mustn't let anyone see the list. We don't want our plans falling into the wrong hands.'

'I shall guard it with my life, sir,' Barney said, giving me a salute.

'Very good. We should synchronise our watches,' I suggested.

'What does that mean?'

'It means we set them for the same time as each other,' I explained. 'Then we can plan a time for the expedition to leave on Saturday.'

'What time will it be?' he asked.

'How about oh-nine-hundred,' I said.

'Nine hundred what?'

I laughed. 'That's the time we're going to leave, you dope. Nine o'clock.'

'Oh. Nine hundred.'

'Right,' I said. 'And the other thing we have to decide is who's going to be the captain.'

'It's my vessel, so *I'm* the captain,' said Barney, as if this was the most obvious thing in the world.

'Okay, and I'll be the navigator. But you'd better learn how to tell the time before Saturday. I reckon Captain Cook at least knew how to tell the time.'

'Captain Cook was murdered by the Americans,' Barney replied, as if that was supposed to be some kind of excuse for him not knowing how to tell the time properly.

'Captain Cook was killed by the Hawaiians,' I corrected him. 'Who weren't Americans then.'

'Whatever. He still died.'

I decided to let that one go.

I rang Barney on Friday night. His brother Tom answered the phone. 'All set for the big adventure?' he asked me.

'It's just a camping trip,' I said, trying to sound casual.

'Not planning on doing any fishing?'

'Fishing? Oh, I don't know. We might,' I said. 'Why do you ask?'

Tom sounded like he was about to laugh. 'Or are you just going to concentrate on the reconnoitre of Black Swamp? I hear that it's in desperate need of a good reconnoitre. Ask anyone.'

'I think you'd better put Barney on,' I said.

A short while later Barney picked up the phone. 'Hello.'

'Guard it with your life, eh?' I said, cutting him off. 'So I guess your life's not worth much.'

'What?'

'The list. Has Tom seen it? Because he's talking about fishing, and reconnoitring —'

'He found it.'

'Where?'

'On the kitchen table.'

I sighed. 'You're not really cut out for this secretive thing, are you?'

'I guess not,' he admitted. 'So what did you ring for? Mum's about to wash my hair ... iest, manliest jumper, and I have to help her. Make sure it doesn't shrink.'

'She's about to *what*? Oh, never mind,' I said. 'So we're still on for tomorrow?'

'You bet,' Barney replied. 'We're going to catch him, you know. We're going to catch Big Red. I've got this feeling.'

'We're only going for two days.'

'I know, but like I said, I've got this feeling. It's kind of tingly, in my spine.'

'You sure that's not your mum washing your hair?'

I could hear the frown in his voice. 'Goodbye, Liam,' he said. 'I'll see you in the morning.'

I got up pretty early the next day. Mum

and Dad were still asleep, but I went in and said goodbye. I got a kiss from Mum, but Dad murmured something about duffers drowning before rolling onto his side.

Otto and I reached Barney's place about seven-thirty. After we'd helped Tom lift the canoe onto the top of his car, we loaded the provisions into the back.

'Barnabus! Barnabus!' Barney's mum called as we were getting into the car. She came down the front steps in her dressing gown, holding a little red parcel. 'The first-aid kit,' she said, poking it through the window at Barney. 'And be careful, love,' she added, giving him a kiss on the cheek.

'I will, Mum,' he said, wiping his face with the back of his hand. 'Come on, Tom, let's go before she does that again.'

I couldn't help laughing when Otto jumped up on him and started licking him all over his face. 'He likes the smell of your shampoo,' I said, which earned me a rather filthy look by way of reply.

It took us about fifteen minutes to drive to our launching place, and we had the canoe loaded and ready to go by eight-thirty. It was pretty full, but it still floated fairly high in the water. 'All right, lads, off you go then,' said Tom, standing on the bank with his hands in his pockets. 'I'm sure there's plenty of reconnoitring to do.'

'Oh, we're not leaving until o'ninety clock,' said Barney.

Tom laughed. 'Until *when*?'

'He means oh-nine-hundred,' I explained.

'But you're packed. Why not go now?' Tom asked.

I didn't want to tell him that it was an expedition. 'High tide,' I said, nodding at him, one seafarer to another.

Tom bent down and scratched Otto behind the ears. 'High tide. Right.' Then, with a laugh and a shake of his head, he got into his car, waved once and drove away, leaving us there beside the mirror-surfaced water, the silence settling over us like a clear mist.

Barney and I stood on the bank looking at the loaded canoe. It felt like we did that for ages, just standing by the water, checking our watches from time to time. Finally Barney said, 'How long now?'

I looked at my watch. 'Eight more minutes,' I said.

'Should we …?'

'Yeah, let's go,' I agreed, reaching for my paddle.

'Wait. Before you get in, there's something we have to do,' Barney said, and reaching into his bag he pulled out a bottle of ginger beer.

'What's that for?' I asked.

'To launch our vessel,' he said.

'Are you going to break the bottle over her nose?'

Barney laughed. 'That's a bit violent, isn't it? I thought I might just pour it over the front. What do you think?'

'Sounds like a good idea.'

'Can you say something official-sounding?' he asked.

'Like what?'

'Like something you'd say if you were the prime minister, and you were launching a great ship.'

'Oh, okay,' I said, thinking. 'Okay, I think I've got something.' I cleared my throat. 'Dearly beloved, we are gathered here today —'

'It's not a funeral.'

'Okay then, try this. Dear friends —'

'Do you have to say 'dear' anything? It sounds a bit ... I don't know. Churchy, I guess.'

'You say something then,' I suggested. 'You're the one holding the champagne anyway.'

'Good point. All right then, here we go. 'Ladies and gentlemen, honoured guests, dogs, it is with great pleasure that I launch this mighty vessel, and name her ...' What did we call it again?'

'*Stoutheart*,' I said.

'I name her *Stoutheart*. God bless her and the souls that sail upon her.'

'That's pretty good,' I said.

'Thanks. I read it in a book.' Barney unscrewed the lid from the ginger beer and poured it over the front of the canoe. 'So now it's official.'

'It feels right, now,' I said. 'Like you say, official.'

Formalities out of the way, and with Otto perched on the very tip of the bow sniffing the morning air and licking at the ginger beer, we pushed off and paddled away from the shore. It was so quiet — just a few birds singing in the bush, and a kookaburra chuckling way off in the distance. The only other sound was the water bubbling under the front of the canoe, and the regular splish and dribble as we paddled across the glassy surface.

'Where to, Mr Navigator?' Barney asked from his position at the stern.

'That way,' I said, pointing upriver. 'I think we should go that way.'

'Very good, sir,' he said, bringing the bow slowly around. 'No, wait, I'm the captain, so you should be calling *me* "sir".'

'Whatever,' I replied. 'The Hawaiians can eat you first, then.'

The coolness of the morning soon burnt away under the summer sun, and after maybe half an hour of steady paddling we had to stop and take off our jackets.

'How much further?' Barney asked, wiping the sweat from his face.

I shrugged. 'How much further do you want to go? We're exploring, after all.'

'Have you been drawing the maps?'

'Do I look like I've been drawing maps? I've been paddling my bum off!'

'So have I! You're not the only one who's been paddling!'

'I know, just ... Shush!' I said suddenly, for just off to the right, in the shadow of a dead log, I'd seen a splash. It wasn't a big splash, little more than a disturbance in the water, but definitely some kind of movement. 'Did you see that?' I asked as Otto sat up straight, his ears and eyes focused on the spot.

'Yeah, I saw it,' Barney whispered. 'Do you think it was him? Do you think it was Big Red?'

I felt myself shiver with excitement as the ripples spread across the water towards us. 'I don't know,' I replied, 'but I think we've found our campsite. Just over there near that big white tree looks like a good spot. What do you think, Captain?'

'Looks okay,' he said.

'I reckon we should go over there and unpack the canoe.'

'Yeah, and get the fishing gear and come straight back over here.'

I shook my head. 'I think we should get the camp set up first. Every expedition needs a base camp, and we won't feel like doing it later.'

Barney reluctantly agreed, and began to steer the canoe towards the bank, glancing back over his shoulder at the place where we'd seen the movement in the water. 'It was quite a big splash,' he said, several times. 'Do you think it was Big Red?'

I shrugged. 'It's as good a clue as we've seen, don't you think?'

'I reckon it was Big Red.'

It's amazing how fast you can get a boring job done when there's something more exciting waiting for when you've finished. We had the camp set up in no time flat, and I was in the tent organising my bed when I heard Barney talking to someone. (He doesn't know that I know, but sometimes he pretends that he's a documentary-maker, and he does the voice-over for whatever he's doing at the time. Once I even heard him explaining in a serious voice why Otto was sniffing Mrs Davidson's dog's bum, except I think he had it all wrong. That *couldn't* be the reason — could it?)

I couldn't quite hear what Barney was saying, but pretty soon I knew that he wasn't playing film-makers, because I heard a second voice. It was a man's voice, and it wasn't one that I recognised. Besides, Otto was barking, and Otto doesn't usually bark at Barney, no matter how stupidly he's behaving.

I stuck my head out of the tent. Otto was leaning forward, his ears flat against his head, and he was making a very low growl in the back of his throat. Over by the edge of our clearing was a tall man. He was dressed in a cammo vest, and carried a long, shiny rifle. 'That your dog?' he asked, each word deliberate and slow, his voice deep and gravelly.

'Might be,' Barney replied warily. 'Why?'

'Well, he's not real friendly, is he?' the man said. 'You do know that you're not supposed to have dogs in a state reserve, don't you?'

'Otto, get here!' I snapped, and he came

around behind me and looked out from behind my legs. He was still growling, and the hair along the back of his neck had risen into a little bristly ridge. 'I don't think you're allowed to have guns in here either,' I said to the man. 'You'd better not let my dad see you with it – he's just gone to the toilet and he'll be back soon. *And* he knows the park ranger.'

'Does he indeed? The park ranger? Which one – Dave or Warren?'

'Uh … both,' I said.

The man stared at me. He didn't say anything for a moment. Then: 'All right, I'll tell you what. You keep your dog under control and I'll do the same with this.' He gave a kind of half-smile as he patted his rifle, which looked so hard and real. 'Then we'll all get along just fine. You have a nice night now.' And with that, he glanced at our canoe before wandering off into the bush.

We waited until the cracking of the sticks under his boots had died away before we so much as took a breath. 'Whoa,' said Barney in a low voice. 'Who was that?'

'I don't know, but I didn't like him very much.' The dog began to head off after the man. 'Otto, come here,' I called. When he heard my voice, he stopped and stood all watchdog-like and brave at the edge of the clearing.

'I don't feel like sleeping here any more,' Barney said, glancing around at every tiny sound that came out of the bush.

'I know,' I agreed. 'I know.' I didn't really want to camp out there with a spooked-out Barney. I mean, it was only the middle of the day, and he was already looking for ghosts. But packing up and running off home didn't seem like much of an option either. 'We'll be all right, mate,' I said. 'Anyway, we've got Otto.'

'Otto's only a dog, and not even a very big one,' Barney said. 'What's he going to do against a gun?'

'He won't have to do anything, because

that guy won't even come back,' I said. 'He was scared when I told him that my dad knows the ranger.'

'Both of them.'

'Yes. Bringing a dog into the reserve is one thing, but that guy would go to jail for bringing a rifle in here.'

'Yeah, I suppose so,' said Barney, but he didn't look very convinced. 'All right then, but at the first sign of trouble—'

'You'll what?' I asked. 'Go home? In the middle of the night? In a canoe?'

Barney frowned. 'I guess you're right. All right, we'll stay, but if I get shot dead, I'll never forgive you.'

'No kidding,' I said.

Chapter 4

Even though it had turned into a beautiful warm day by then, it didn't feel like such a welcoming place any more, once we'd seen the man with the rifle. Being back on the water seemed like a much safer place to be, so we left our campsite in a bit of a mess and threw our rods into the canoe.

We paddled across to where we'd seen the splash earlier. Of course, once we reached the spot there was nothing to see. Nothing except the dead log, with its end sticking out of the water, all mossy and damp.

'What are the chances anyway?' Barney said from the back of the canoe. 'Bailey's Swamp is a pretty big place.'

'Yeah, I know, but you've got to start looking somewhere, don't you?'

We paddled slowly around the log and a little farther along the bank, peering down into the dark water and amongst the grass and reeds and the rocks and dead sticks.

'This is stupid,' said Barney after a while.

'It's not stupid!' I twisted in my seat and glared at him. 'I thought you wanted to come out here and explore.'

'I did. I do.'

'Then start behaving like an explorer!' I snapped. 'What if Columbus had said "This is stupid" the minute the Spanish coast was out of sight?'

'I'm not Columbus – I'm cold.' A cloud drifted across the sun. 'I didn't bring a jacket.'

'What, at all?'

'No, I've got one back at the tent.'

'Then we'll go back and get it, Mr This-Is-Stupid-And-I'm-Cold.'

He looked over his shoulder at our little camp, way back on the opposite bank. 'All right,' he said. 'All right, let's go back.'

He'd just dipped the tip of his paddle in the water when we heard a sound, a bit like someone breaking a dry stick, followed by an echo. It came from the bush beyond our campsite.

'Jeepers creepers!' I said. 'Was that a gunshot?'

'I don't know – what's a gunshot sound like?'

'Just like that!'

'Oh, that does it — I definitely don't want to sleep here tonight.' Barney was shaking his head. 'Can we go home now?'

'No, we can't go home,' I replied.

'Why not?'

'Because it's too late to take the tent and everything down, get it packed away and paddle back. We have to stay here tonight.'

Barney looked like he might start crying any minute, and I noticed that his lips were thin and pale. 'Mate, I'm really scared. They're shooting at stuff up there.'

'Yeah, probably old tin cans,' I said, but I didn't even believe that myself. Not for a minute. 'Listen, we have to go back to camp, have something to eat, go to bed early, and we'll head off first thing in the morning. All right? We'll be fine. All right?'

Barney shook his head.

'Look, mate, we don't have a choice!' I tried to explain. 'Even if we went back to where Tom dropped us off, how are we going to get home?'

'We can walk.'

'With a canoe? No, I vote we stay here, and take off at first light.'

'Okay, but I don't think I'm going to sleep at all,' Barney said. 'I'd never even *seen* a gun before today.'

'I have, heaps of times,' I boasted, but

that wasn't really true. One of the kids in my big brother's class had an air rifle that he showed me once, and it wasn't even loaded. Other than that, a gun was as new to me as it was to Barney.

After a bit of discussion we decided that if we weren't going to go home we might as well do what we'd come for, and fish for Big Red, but we didn't get a single bite. The clouds had cleared from in front of the sun, so all we got was sunburnt necks.

Later, as the sun was dropping low behind the sandstone cliffs lining the opposite side of the river, and just as our stomachs were beginning to make strange hungry noises, Barney said, 'There — look.'

'Look at what?' I asked.

'Smoke,' he replied, pointing just beyond the next bend downriver.

I looked. A thin column of smoke was rising into the clear late-afternoon air. 'That must be their camp,' I said. 'And do you know what that means?'

'That they're camping?' Barney suggested.

'No.'

'That they're cold?'

'No, it means —'

'That they're making their dinner?'

'Will you stop? It means that they're settling in for the night. Once you've got a fire burning, you're not going anywhere. That's kind of a camping rule.'

'Should *we* have a fire?' Barney asked.

'Of course!' I said. 'What's a camp without a fire?'

'Harder to find at night, that's what.'

Then we had a conversation that I don't think I can write down here, because we both said a few things that we probably would never have said under normal circumstances. But these were not normal circumstances. Otto knew it, too. He was sitting like a statue at the front of the canoe, totally focused on the column of smoke in the distance, just a thin line of white rising and swaying up into the sky.

Finally Barney won the 'Will we have a fire or not?' conversation. I think he thought he won it because he was the captain. Really I just gave in because he looked like he was going to start crying if he didn't get his way. And when Barney cries (which I think he does a little bit too often, to be honest) it's quite embarrassing to watch, all dribbling nose and wobbly chin, and nothing at all like Captain Cook would have done. So to save all that, I gave in. We wouldn't have a fire.

Think of the most dissatisfying meal you've ever eaten. Now imagine it even less satisfying, add some coldness, darkness and a good pinch of fear, and that was what our dinner was like. We squatted on a couple of damp logs and ate cold baked beans on bread in silence, our ears hearing every tiny noise from the bush, while Otto sat at the edge of our little clearing and growled softly into the darkening bush.

Barney broke the silence first. 'Oh dear.'

'What?'

'My toothbrush. I forgot it. Mum's going to kill me!'

I shook my head. Perhaps Barney wasn't really cut out for this exploring caper after all. It definitely seemed a shame to be camping without a fire, but somehow the gloss had already been taken off the trip once we'd seen the man with the gun anyway.

'This is a washout,' I said. 'I think I might go to bed.'

'What? And leave me out here?' Barney whimpered.

'You know, if you'd let us have a fire, *sir*, there'd be something to stay up for. But since you won't —'

I was interrupted by the sound of another gunshot from up the river, followed by a low growl from Otto.

'Crikey!' said Barney. His eyes were wide in the semi-darkness. 'We've got to get out of here. I can't sleep in that tent. I mean it this time — I can't stay here.' His voice was terrified and pleading.

I looked up at the night sky. The stars were starting to prick through, and a half-moon was low in the north-east. There'd be enough light to paddle by, and once we were back at our starting point we could spend what was left of the night there. But packing up a camp at night? What if we left something valuable behind, or broke some important piece of equipment, like a leg?

Then the sharp crack of another shot echoed off the cliffs, and my mind was suddenly made up. Barney was right. We couldn't stay there. 'Okay,' I agreed, 'I'm with you. Let's just go.'

If you think you can get a camp set up fast if there's something you want to get to, you should see how fast you can pull a camp *down* if you're scared of something. *Gunfire* scared, I mean. When I was much younger I read books about kids running away from ghosts, giant spiders, axe-wielding maniacs, and they were a bit scary, I suppose. But those things never felt real. But when real gunshots start ringing out of the real darkness, *then* you know what fear really is. Lip-biting, eye-watering, chest-squeezing fear.

'That wind's starting to pick up,' I said, as we loaded the last of the gear into the canoe. 'It's a headwind. Paddling back is going to be hard work.'

'I don't care,' Barney replied.

'I think it's going to storm,' I said, glancing at the building clouds.

'I don't care.'

'There might be lightning.'

Barney stopped and looked at me. 'What? Lightning?'

'Yes, you know — flashes of electricity, usually with thunder.'

'Stop mucking around, Liam! I know what lightning is. But do we want to be on the water in a thunderstorm?'

'With aluminium paddles,' I added.

'Now you're just trying to scare me.'

I shook my head. I really wasn't. 'I'm just saying, it's not completely safe out there either. It's not too late to unpack the tent if you want to stay.'

Just then we heard another shot ring out from the bush.

Barney's chin had started to wobble. 'Oh … *farts*,' he said. 'Farts and wee and … and *farts*.'

'It's your call, Captain,' I said.

Barney was looking at the sky, then glancing over his shoulder in the direction of the gunshots. 'Oh, I don't know,' he said. 'What do you think?'

'It only looks like wind for now,' I said. 'I say we start, and if the storm comes for real, we find somewhere to stop and shelter. We don't even need the tent — we've got the groundsheet.'

'All right, that sounds like a good plan,' Barney agreed. 'Let's go.'

'Where's Otto?' I said, looking around. 'Did you see where he went?'

'No.'

'Otto! Otto, come here,' I called. 'Come back, buddy. It's time to go.'

'Don't worry, he'll catch up,' said Barney, picking up his paddle and edging towards the canoe.

I stared at my friend. Was he serious? 'How's he going to catch up? He can hardly swim across the bath!'

'He'll go through the bush. He's a dog. They can find their way home from heaps far away. I saw this thing on telly once —'

'We're not leaving him behind! I have to find him! Where's the torch? Otto! Otto!'

Barney started swearing again as I grabbed the torch and headed off towards the bush. I mean, it's not like I *wanted* to go into the dark shadows amongst the trees and shrubs and dead logs, but Otto was my dog, and my responsibility. And he was my friend, too.

I didn't think he could be far away. Otto hates storms, and by that I mean he *really* hates them. And he doesn't wait until they actually start before he gets scared – he can sense a storm half an hour or more before it begins. The first thing that happens is he starts growling. Then his ears go flat and he starts to look worried. Next comes the lying as flat as he can on the ground, and after that it's the slinking along on his belly looking for a hole or a hiding place of any kind. Under my bedclothes is his favourite, or under the couch. At that moment, as it hit me that Otto wasn't there, it also hit me that our couch and my bed were too far away for my liking, too.

'Well, this is just *great*!' Barney said. 'Exactly what we need — your stupid dog running away.'

'He's not stupid!' I retorted. 'He's just scared, that's all.'

'Yeah? Well, so am I.'

'That's just too bad, isn't it? Are you coming?'

'In there?' Barney said, pointing at the

bush.

'Yes, in there.'

He shook his head. 'No way.'

'Okay then, you stay here, and I'll go and find him.'

'What? Stay here? By myself? While you go in there? Without me?'

I put my hands on my hips and glared at him. 'Well, which one is it going to be, Barney?' No one was calling anyone 'sir' anymore. 'Are you coming or staying?'

Barney made a frustrated kind of sound in the back of his throat and said, 'All right, but if we die —'

'Yeah, yeah, I know, you'll never forgive me.'

'Exactly.'

'Fine, whatever. What are you bringing that for?' I asked as he walked towards me carrying his paddle.

'This? It's a weapon.'

I stared at him some more. He stared back at me. We didn't say anything for a long

moment. Then: 'Excellent idea,' I said. 'I'll
get mine as well.'

Chapter 5

One of the problems with making a list before going camping is that you only take what's on your list. And since there was only one torch on our list, one torch was all we had. That was how Barney and I ended up sneaking through the bush with our shoulders pressed close together, arguing about where the beam of light from my torch should be pointing. 'Over there,' Barney would say, and I'd say, 'What's that? Otto, is that you?' and move the torch. Then

Barney would catch his paddle on something, or he'd trip. 'How can I even see where I'm going if you won't point the light over here?' he'd say, and I'd ignore him because I'd hear a rustle from the undergrowth and swing the torch in that direction. And on it went, me calling to Otto, Barney whining.

After what felt like at least half an hour of fairly aimless searching, with thunder and occasional gunshots in the distance and Barney constantly telling me to keep my voice down, we reached a fire trail. We jumped down from the bank at the edge and stood in the middle of it, our torch beam flickering across the bush and the bank on the opposite side of the trail, and the cold, dry gravel under our feet. I felt like someone had stuck a pin in me and let all my air out. In fact, I felt like *I* wanted to get all chin-wobbly myself. 'Great. What do we do now?' I muttered. 'Otto's gone. I think he's really gone.'

We stood there, turning in circles as a low rumble in the sky reminded us that the weather was still closing in.

'Liam, listen to me. We don't have a choice,' Barney said. 'We have to go back to the camp. We have to. Anyway, maybe your dog's gone back there and is waiting for us.'

I would have agreed with him, except I couldn't speak. So instead I just nodded.

'Cool. Let's go.' He grabbed the torch and started walking towards the bush at the side of the track.

'Wait,' I said. 'The camp's this way. You're going in the wrong direction.'

'No,' Barney replied. 'That's the way we were going, and now we're heading back.'

'What? No, *this* is the way back, *that's* the way we were going. The moon is over there …' I pointed at the sky, but when I saw that the clouds had closed in completely now, and the moon was totally obscured, I felt my stomach sink.

'So which way is it?' said Barney, turning

around a few more times, with the torch flashing across trees, trees and more trees. 'We came out near that one there,' he said.

'No, we came out near *that* one, I'm sure of it.'

We stood and stared at each other. The torch beam was reflecting weirdly under his chin, turning his eyes into dark, deep holes in his face. 'So,' he said, 'does this mean that we're lost, Mr Navigator?'

Lost? How could we be lost standing in the middle of a fire trail that we'd walked onto just a few minutes before? I looked around again, just in case there was some feature that I'd missed, some strange branch or bush or rock I might have seen when we first came onto the track.

'We're not lost,' I said, with a lot more confidence than I felt.

'Aren't we?'

'No. We ... we just don't know exactly where we are.'

'Oh,' Barney said. 'Well, it's good to know

that we're not lost.'

'Barney,' I said.

'Yes, Liam?'

'I think we're lost.'

'Okay, and I've been thinking about this,' Barney said, very calmly. 'It's either that way or that way, isn't it?'

'You're right — it's really just the toss of a coin.'

'Except we don't have a coin,' Barney replied.

'It's a figure of …' Another rifle shot came from the bush to my left. 'Crikey, that one was close. Well, at least we know which way we should be going now,' I said, turning to my right. 'Away from that.'

We set off into the bush again, still calling Otto, and trying not to worry about the way our torch beam was rapidly fading.

'Shouldn't we be there by now?' Barney asked after a bit. 'We've been heading this way for a while now.'

'We know that we'll get to the water

eventually,' I replied. 'If we just keep going, that is.'

But how long do you keep going in one direction before you accept that you're lost again? We didn't get a chance to find out, because the thunder was getting louder and closer, and there were flashes of lightning in the clouds every minute or so. After his brief moment of pulling himself together, Barney was starting to look frightened again.

Then the rain started, heavy drops thwacking into the dirt at our feet, and rustling through the leaves of the trees. 'This is getting really unpleasant now,' Barney complained. 'I was cold before, and now I'm wet and cold. And I think the torch battery is getting flat.'

'Barney.'

'Yes, Liam?'

'I'm getting wet and cold too, okay? So can you please —'

'Be quiet,' Barney muttered.

'Exactly. Can you just be quiet for one minute —'

'No, I mean you be quiet,' Barney said. He'd stopped walking, and was pointing into the dark shadows of the bush. 'I thought I heard a noise, just over there.'

I stood close behind him, and together we peered into the darkness. 'It's probably a possum or something,' I whispered. 'A wombat, maybe.'

But then, without warning, the torch beam went out, as quickly as if its switch had been pressed. I was about to say something whingy, when Barney said in a very low voice, 'Look there. Did you see the light?'

'What light?'

'There was a flash of light through those trees there. It looked like a torch or something —'

His voice was interrupted by the sound of a rifle shot, very close by, and in the exact direction we were facing. Without a thought, we both dropped to our faces in the mud and sticks.

'Is it the same guy we saw this afternoon?' Barney whispered.

'How would I know?'

'Oh, I'm not happy, mate,' said Barney. 'I think I might have just wet my pants.'

'I know how you feel,' I replied.

'What do we do now?'

'Shh — I think I hear someone,' I said. I was sure I'd heard a man's voice, deep and slow and gravelly, although I couldn't make out what he'd said.

We both crouched there and listened. Then I heard it for sure, and this time I could understand some of the words.

'What did you do with that dog?' the voice said.

'I got rid of it, like you said,' a second voice replied. 'So it wouldn't get in the way, barking and carrying on.'

'Good. No problem?'

'Dead easy. No bother at all. Hardly made a squeak.'

I was so angry. 'They've killed Otto!' I

whispered, barely able to hold back my sobs.

'I know,' Barney said. 'Shh, I can't hear what they're saying.'

'Had enough for one night?' the first man asked.

'Yeah, I think so,' the other one replied. 'I'd like to get back before this rain gets any heavier.'

'What about the ones you saw down near the water earlier?'

'No, we'll go back for them tomorrow. They're not causing any trouble for now. We know where they are, and I'm pretty sure that's their usual spot. They'll be there in the morning.'

By this stage Barney and I had gone back to lying flat on the ground, our hearts thumping so loudly I was sure that the men would hear them over the sound of the rain and wind through the leaves. We lay there for a very long time, neither of us game to say a word for fear of catching the men's attention. This also gave me time to have a quiet cry for my brave little dog Otto, who'd run off to defend us and was now dead.

Finally, after the men's voices had died away, Barney whispered to me, 'Do you think they're gone?'

'I think so. I hope so,' I replied.

'Did you hear that man's voice? It was definitely the man we saw at our camp.'

'You're right,' I answered. 'I didn't like him then, and I sure don't like him now.'

'So, do you still want to stick around until morning?' Barney asked.

'No way! As soon as we find our camp, we get out of here. We've got to tell someone what's happening. We've got to get in that canoe and start paddling, tonight. I vote we leave behind anything we haven't already packed.'

'Sounds good to me. Hey, did you hear that?' Barney said, for about the hundredth time since we'd started looking for poor Otto.

'Did I hear what?' I asked.

That was when, from behind us, we heard the gravelly-voiced man whisper, 'Troy, over here. You come around that side.'

'Okay,' the other man answered from in front of us. 'Don't shoot me, though.'

'Yeah, well, be ready if they decide to run at you.'

Barney and I froze, right there on our stomachs in the undergrowth. I could hear Barney's breath coming out in short, terrified pants. Or was that my breath I could hear? A kind of deep, sinking chill ran all the way through my body. I wanted to burst into tears, or scream, or jump up and run, or something. But in the end, all I could do was squeeze my eyes shut as hard as I could, maybe hoping that when I reopened them I'd be back in our tent, or, better still, in my bed back home, with Otto sleeping at my feet.

'Now,' said a voice, and suddenly we were bathed in bright light. There was a

click as one of the men cocked his rifle.

'Stop, stop!' shouted the one behind us. 'Troy, it's kids!'

'What? Kids? Crikey, I almost —'

'Please don't hurt us!' I yelled, standing up with my hands raised. 'We're just kids! We're just kids! We won't tell anyone if you just let us go!'

'What? We're not going to hurt you,' said the one called Troy from behind the blinding beam of light shining into my face. I heard him uncock his rifle.

'But we heard you before,' I explained. 'You said you were going to get us in the morning.'

'What?'

'We heard you. You said you'd come back for us in the morning.'

'What? I don't remember saying that,' Troy said. 'Kenny, did we say that?'

'I don't think so,' said Kenny.

'What were you talking about, then? You said you saw us down by the water.'

'Not you!' Kenny replied. 'We meant a couple of feral pigs we saw down there earlier. That's why we're out here – we're hunting feral pigs. That's what we thought you were just now, scratching about in the undergrowth. We almost shot you, you crazy kids!'

'Hey, Barney,' I said, almost laughing with relief. 'Barney, they thought we were pigs.' I looked down at my friend. He was squirming in the mud, his eyes squeezed shut just like mine had been a moment ago. 'Barney, get up!'

'I can't,' he said.

'Why not?'

'I think I've really wet myself this time.'

Chapter 6

'You could have shot us!' I shouted at the men, once I'd caught my breath and made sure that I hadn't wet myself as well.

'Yeah, and anyway, guns are illegal in a state reserve,' Barney added, holding his hands in front of his pants as he got slowly to his feet. 'We told you that when you came to our camp,' he said to the tall man, Kenny.

'And we told you, we're hunting,' Kenny answered. 'But that doesn't explain why *you're* out here. You're a long way from your camp, which is in *that* direction, by the way.'

'We were camping, and then we had to look for our dog,' I said. 'He ran away.'

'Your dog, huh? Little guy, white, brown patch on his back?' asked Kenny.

'Jack Russell terrier?' said Troy.

'Yeah, that's the one,' I said. 'He wasn't a fancy show dog or anything, but he was *my* dog. And I don't care if you're out here hunting man-eating lions, you can't just going around killing people's pets.'

'Killing pets?' Troy shook his head. 'No one killed anyone's pet, unless your pet is a feral pig.'

'But we heard you before. You said that you'd taken care of him.'

'And we *did* take care of him. Come with us and we'll show you.'

Barney and I looked at each other. This was almost definitely a bad idea, even though we now felt satisfied that these men weren't planning to shoot us. Besides, we were hopelessly lost anyway.

'It's just through there,' Kenny said. 'Your dog's safe. Come on, come and see.'

Barney and I brushed ourselves off. 'All right,' I said reluctantly. 'But if you're lying to us —'

'We're not,' said Troy. 'Scout's honour.'

'As if *that's* going to make any difference,' Barney muttered.

We followed the men through the bush, their torches bobbing about and making strange, dancing shadows leap through the bush. While we walked, Kenny told us more about what he and Troy were doing there. 'The National Parks Service hired us to cull the feral pig population around Bailey's Swamp,' he explained.

'What's so bad about a couple of pigs?' Barney asked.

Kenny snorted. 'More like a couple of hundred. Don't be fooled; they do a lot of damage to the native animals and plants. Better off dead.'

'Isn't it cruel?' I asked.

'What, culling pigs? No, not especially. One shot, bang, it's all over. Besides, they're a pest, and like I said, they harm the animals that should be here.'

'So you're paid to shoot stuff?' I asked.

'Basically, yes,' said Kenny.

'Cool,' said Barney, who seemed to be getting over his earlier anxiety.

Soon we reached the men's campsite. Parked beside a couple of small tents and a camp-kitchen was a four-wheel-drive ute, with a tarp over the back of it. In the dim light from the gas light burning beside the kitchen I saw a pig's trotter poking out from under the edge of the tarp.

'How many pigs have you shot?' I asked.

'Dunno, exactly,' said Kenny. 'Hey Troy, how many have we taken?'

I didn't hear Troy's reply, because I'd just heard a high-pitched whimper. It was Otto, who was tied to the bullbar of the ute. He was tugging on his rope, trying to get to me,

yelping and whining.

'Otto!' I shouted, and I was in such a rush to get to my dog that I tripped over a root hiding in the shadows at my feet and fell flat on my face. Scrambling back up, I ran over to hug him. 'I thought you were dead,' I said as he licked my face. 'Where did you run away to? And what's this you've got here?' I poked at a well-gnawed bone at my feet. 'Where did you get this?'

'He sure likes feral pig, that little guy,' said Kenny, who had come over and was standing behind me. 'I hope you don't mind.' He bent down and scratched the top of Otto's head. 'Good tucker, isn't it, mate?'

'He's a terrier. Mum says they'll eat anything.'

'Well, he sure likes pig. Do you boys want some hot chocky or something before we take you back to your camp? Troy's just putting the kettle on.'

'Yes, please,' I said. 'I'm really tired. What time is it?'

Kenny shone his torch onto his watch. 'Oh, look at that,' he said. 'It's only half past eight.'

Even though he'd been really happy to see me, I don't think Otto was all that pleased to be leaving Kenny and Troy's campsite. I suppose that when you're a dog, being fed bits of dead pig that was live pig an hour or two before isn't such a bad way to spend an evening.

'Are you two going to be all right?' Kenny asked us, once he'd walked us back to our site. Somehow he'd found his way through the bush in the darkness without following any kind of clear path.

'We'll have to pitch our tent again,' I said, 'but I think we can do that all right. At least the rain's gone.'

'Our torch is flat,' Barney reminded me.

'Here,' Kenny said, holding out his torch. 'Borrow mine, and I'll come and get it in the morning.'

'How will you get back to Troy?' I asked.

Kenny glanced at the moon, which was trying to come out from behind a cloud. 'I'll be all right. Here, take it.'

'Thanks,' I said.

'No worries. See you in the morning.'

If taking a camp down in the dark is tricky, setting it up in the dark is way trickier. But eventually we had our tent pitched and our sleeping bags laid out. 'That'll do,' I said. 'Let's just go to bed, and we can get the breakfast stuff out in the morning.'

'Good idea,' said Barney.

We lay awake in our tent, listening to the sounds of the bush. It all seemed so much less scary, now that we knew the reason for the gunshots we'd heard.

'Hey, Liam.'

'What?'

'Were you scared?'

'Me? No, not really. I knew there had to be an explanation.'

'No, I wasn't scared either. I didn't really

wet my pants, you know.'

'No?'

'No. It was just a puddle. I lay down right in a puddle.'

'Did you?'

'Yep, that's all it was.'

'Cool.'

There was silence again for a while. Then: 'Hey, Liam.'

'What?'

'Should we tell our parents about —'

'No. No, not for a while, I reckon.'

'Yeah, that's what I thought too. Hey, Liam.'

'What?'

'Are we going to go fishing for Big Red in the morning?'

'No. I want to go home. I think Otto's getting homesick.'

'Yeah, I thought that too. He looks pretty homesick.'

Again there was silence. Then I said, 'Hey, Barney.'

Nothing.
'Hey, Barney.'
But Barney was asleep.

Chapter 7

I'd be lying if I said that I had a great night's sleep. Weird dreams, strange noises and Barney muttering in his sleep woke me up several times. Once I didn't know where I was and lay there frowning at the tent fabric, wondering how I'd come to be there. But between the interruptions, I did sleep a bit.

I woke up in what felt like a sauna. The sun was beating down on the tent, making everything inside glow a weird pink colour.

Right above us, a kookaburra was having a huge laugh. When I looked over at Barney, I saw that he was still fast asleep, snoring gently. I unzipped my sleeping bag to give my sweaty feet some air, and Otto yawned and stretched at the end of my bed.

It was a beautiful morning down there by the glassy water of Bailey's Swamp. It seemed hard to believe that all those horrible experiences of the night before had happened in such a lovely, peaceful place. In fact, I was starting to wonder if it had really been as frightening as all that.

With Otto exploring close by, I gathered some wood from the bush, trying to find some sticks that weren't too wet. Eventually, using a bit of our roll of toilet paper as dry kindling, I managed to make a small, very smoky fire. Once it was going well enough, I went down to the canoe to get the box of food.

It was while I was carrying the food back up to the tent that I heard Otto barking in the distance. I looked up. He was about a hundred metres away, and barely more than a tiny white spot on the end of a small outcrop of rocks jutting into the water. He was barking like mad at something in the water.

'Otto, what is it?' I called. 'Come on, mate, come back here. I don't want you to run off again.'

'What's he barking at?' asked Barney, who was stretching and rubbing his eyes in the doorway of the tent.

I shrugged. 'Who knows? Probably ducks or something. Baked beans for brekky?'

Barney turned up his nose. 'Again? What about those eggs we brought?'

'Two of them are busted,' I said. 'I think we broke them in the rush to pack up last night.'

Otto was still barking, darting up and down along the rocks, his eyes fixed on the water.

Barney had come all the way out of the

tent now, and was pulling on his jeans. 'Hey, Liam.'

'What?'

'Last night you said you didn't want to go fishing today.'

'Yeah, I know,' I admitted. 'But now that I see what a great day it's turned into —'

'What I mean is, and this might be a stupid idea, but do you think that Otto might be barking at ... at Big Red?'

'Big Red?'

'Big Red.'

'Do you think it could be?'

'Definitely could be,' Barney replied.

'Big Red!' I shouted. 'Quick, grab the stuff.'

We grabbed our fishing gear from the canoe and started running towards Otto. He was still barking, his front paws just in the water's edge and his ears all the way forward. He glanced up as he heard us approaching, then went straight back to barking at the water.

'What is it, Otto? What can you see, mate?' There were no ducks or anything nearby. All the birds had been scared off by the noise he was making, and yet he was still focused on the water. 'Is it a big fish? Is that what you can see?'

'Hang on … there, I saw something,' said Barney, standing close by my shoulder and pointing. 'Did you see it?'

'What am I supposed to have seen?'

'Something orange, deep down.'

'Orange? Are you sure?'

'No, not really. The water's so murky.'

'Otto, shush,' I said. 'If it was orange —'

'There!' said Barney. 'See it?'

That time I saw it too, a very faint and rather large orange tinge in the water. It was hard to say how deep down it was, though.

'Whoa! Man, that's big, whatever it is,' I breathed.

Barney's voice was very low. 'There aren't any crocodiles in Bailey's Swamp, are there?'

'No. And definitely not orange ones. I

think that was a ... Whoa!' I said, interrupting myself as a huge flash of orange drifted by, maybe a metre or more below the surface.

'You should get Otto back from the edge,' Barney said. 'That thing could stick its head out of the water and take him like a killer whale.'

'Otto, shush! Barney, bait a hook,' I said, not taking my eyes from the water for a single second.

'With what?'

'I don't care. Whatever. Just make it the biggest hook you've got, on the heaviest line. And plenty of bait.'

In the time it took Barney to finish rigging the gear, I saw the orange shadow three or four times. Finally I felt the rod pressed into my hand.

'That's the heaviest line I've got,' Barney said.

'I just hope it's heavy enough. Here you go, Mr Red,' I said, as I cast over the spot where I'd last seen the underwater shape. 'Come and get some brekky.'

'What if it takes the bait?' Barney asked.

'Then we catch it, obviously.'

'But we don't know how big it is. It could be too big for even that line.'

'If it breaks the line, it breaks the line,' I replied. 'But imagine if we caught Big Red and took it back!'

I looked at Barney. His eyes were huge. 'We'd be heroes,' he said.

'Exactly. Big Red-catching —'

Suddenly my rod bent almost double as the line pulled taut and vibrated like a guitar string.

'I've got a hit!' I shouted.

'Let it run! Let the reel run!' Barney screamed, and I succeeded in getting the catch released before the line could stretch and break. The thin strand tore off through the water with a sharp crackle, leaving a white streak on the glassy surface. Then the streak made a hard left turn as the fish took off parallel to the shore, in the direction of our camp.

'What do I do now?' I asked Barney, who'd done heaps more fishing than me over the years.

'Just let it swim.'

'What if I run out of line?'

'All right, just put a bit of tension on it if you like. But not too much.'

I did as he'd suggested, but the line was still spinning out at a terrifying speed as the rod bent and vibrated in my hands.

'It's not going to work,' I said. 'The line's coming off too fast. I'm going to follow around the bank.'

So Barney and Otto and I went after that crazy orange fish, hopping and stepping and jogging along the bank and the reedy shallows as the fish swam furiously away from us. A couple of times it doubled back towards the shore, and when it did, I took the chance to reel in a bit of line. But then it'd turn and dart off again, and I was back to letting the reel slip so I wouldn't lose the fish altogether.

'Watch the canoe,' Barney warned me as we reached our campsite. 'Don't trip over it.'

'Big Red's running again,' I said, as the rod suddenly jerked and whipped. 'We're going to run out of line for sure. I wish I could walk out there after it, just so I wouldn't have to let so much out.'

'The canoe,' Barney said.

'Okay, I heard you!' I snapped.

'No, mate — get *in* the canoe. I'll paddle after the fish.'

'What? Yeah, good idea,' I said. 'Push it out a bit, then I'll get in the front.'

Barney grabbed his paddle and pushed the canoe off the sandy bank into the water. 'Righto,' he said, holding the rod while I climbed in. Otto was in the canoe in a flash. He wasn't missing out on any of *this* action.

Barney pushed us off, and the rod felt happier straightaway, with Barney taking some of the strain off by paddling after the fish.

'You can slow down a bit,' I said.

'What?'

'I said, you can slow down a bit if you want.'

'What do you mean? I'm hardly paddling at all!'

I looked back at him. It was true — he was barely dipping his paddle into the water. 'So why —'

'Nantucket thingummy,' he said.

'Nantucket sleigh-ride? Do you think?'

'Yeah, I do,' Barney replied with a little shrug. 'Seriously, I'm barely paddling at all.'

'No way,' I breathed, as the bow of the canoe kept on peeling the glassy water apart.

'Way,' said Barney.

Chapter 8

That big orange fish towed us all over that lagoon for more than an hour. It'd tire for a while, and I'd reel it in a bit, then it'd decide it was time to swim some more, and I'd give it some line to play with. Barney was having a great time, sitting at the back of the canoe watching me wrestle with the creature from the deep. He was very encouraging, too: 'I'm getting sunburnt,' and 'I'm thirsty,' and 'How much longer, do you reckon?'

Finally I started to make some progress,

and bit by bit I reeled that fish in. Although I was pretty tired, it seemed that Big Red was exhausted. And at last I wound in a long length of line and saw its orange bulk rising towards me.

'There it is,' Barney said, and Otto started barking.

'Otto, shush! Come on, big fella,' I said to the fish as I reeled in the last bit, and there it was, right next to the canoe, an enormous orange and brown cod, its tail moving slowly, its mouth opening and closing as if it was panting.

Barney was totally awestruck. 'How heavy do you reckon it is?'

'I don't know. It's at least as big as you.'

'Wow!' Barney breathed, shaking his head.

I couldn't help grinning. 'We did it,' I said. 'We actually caught Big Red. I can't believe it!'

'That was so awesome,' said Barney. 'So what do we do now?'

I looked up. We were at least fifty or sixty metres from the shore, and probably half a kilometre upstream from our camp. I wasn't sure how we'd manage to get the fish in to shore, not to mention getting it home so that people could admire it ... and us. 'We'll have to tow it,' I said.

'All the way home?'

'Well, we can't fit it in the canoe along with all our camping gear, can we?'

'So we leave the camping gear behind.'

'We can't do that,' I said. 'That stuff belongs to my parents!'

'Good point. So what do you think we should do?'

We sat and thought for a bit, as Big Red floated beside the canoe, totally spent, and Otto perched at the side, his front paws on the gunwale and his eyes fixed on the fish. His head twisted from side to side, as if he was expecting Big Red to turn into something more edible.

'I know,' I said at last. 'I've got it. We cut

its head off.'

'That's disgusting! Why?'

'If we cut the head off and take that home, everyone will see how big it was, but we won't have to take all of it back.'

'I don't know ...'

'It's the perfect solution,' I said. 'We cut its head off, everyone goes "Wow, that's a huge cod. You boys caught Big Red", and that's it. Heroes. Nantucket sleigh-riding heroes.'

'All right,' Barney said, but he still didn't seem convinced. 'Did you bring the knife?'

'We didn't even unpack it from the canoe,' I said. 'It's right there near your feet.'

'All right, if you really think that's the best thing to do. You make sure it doesn't escape, and I'll paddle us in to shore. We can do the cutting just over there.'

It took us a while, but eventually we grounded onto a little gravelly beach. I climbed over the side, and after a bit of slipping, falling, grasping and sliding, as well as some advice from Otto, we finally got Big

Red up onto dry land.

'Are you sure about this?' Barney said again. He looked sick.

I unsheathed the hunting knife and felt its weight in my hand. 'It's the only way,' I said.

'Well, if it really is the only way ...'

I stepped forward. Big Red's gills were panting open and shut, and it wriggled a bit. Its skin was slick, its black eyes shiny. 'It's all right, mate – this will only take a second,' I told the fish.

'Are you sure about this?' Barney asked yet again.

'Can you stop asking me that?' I said, straightening up.

'But are you?'

I looked at that enormous fish staring up at me, its tail scrabbling lightly at the sand and mud. I'd never even seen a fish as big as that, let alone killed one.

'How old do you reckon it is?' I asked.

Barney shrugged. 'I've got no idea,' he replied. 'How old do fish get?'

I swallowed hard. I didn't want my friend to think that I was a coward. And I didn't want people to scoff in disbelief when I told them that we'd actually caught the legendary Big Red of Bailey's Swamp. But at the same time, I didn't really want to kill this brave old fish, a fish I'd fought for the last couple of hours.

I took a deep breath. It had to be done. So readjusting my grip on the knife, I reached down and cut the fishing line, close to the hook, and pulled out the hook through Big Red's bottom lip. 'Come on, Barney,' I said, 'help me get this old fella back in the water.'

We struggled a bit, but at last we slid the fish over the sand and the final couple of metres into the deeper water as Otto looked at us as if we'd gone completely mad.

For some reason Barney and I didn't look at each other as we nudged the fish forward slightly, and felt its body bend against the water. I still wonder what I would have seen if I had looked at my friend's face. Sadness?

Relief? Happiness? Probably all of those things.

'Go on,' said Barney to the fish. 'Go on, swim away.'

'Yeah, it's okay,' I said. 'It was a good fight, and you know I won, don't you?'

Then Big Red stirred, and with a flick of its tail it became first an orange blur in the water, then nothing at all. It was gone.

'See you, big fella,' I said.

'Yeah, see you, mate,' Barney murmured.

'Who are you talking to?' asked a voice behind us. We turned around. Kenny and Troy were there, cradling their rifles in their arms and smiling.

'Oh, we caught a big fish,' I explained. 'There's this cod that's supposed to be just a legend, but we caught it, and then we let it go. Not that we expect anyone to believe us.'

'It wasn't Big Red, was it?' Kenny asked.

'Do you know about Big Red?' said Barney.

'I'd never seen it until today, but I'd heard about it, sure. Who hasn't?'

'What do you mean, you'd never seen it *until today*? Did you see it?'

'Sure, just then. We saw you let it go. That was pretty decent of you.'

'Yeah, I reckon I'd have kept it,' Troy added. 'Just to brag about.'

'So it's just as well we have the photo as evidence,' said Kenny, and from one of the many pockets in his hunting vest he took a tiny silver digital camera.

I could barely believe it. 'Did you get a photo of Big Red?' I asked.

'Even better,' he answered, and he turned the camera so I could see the little screen at the back. There, clear as anything, was a picture of Barney and me dragging the giant fish out of the water, with Otto encouraging us from the canoe. 'Would a copy of that photo help your friends believe your story?'

'You bet,' I said.

'I think I'm going to wet my pants again,' said Barney.

Chapter 9

We got on the UHF when we were almost at our pickup site, and Barney's brother Tom was waiting for us as we arrived. 'Paddling a bit slow there, boys,' he called as we crept in to shore, our shoulders aching. 'Rough couple of days?'

'You could say that,' said Barney.

'Find anything new?'

'Not really. Nothing we didn't know was there.'

'Catch anything?'

'Not exactly,' I replied. 'Nothing we could keep, anyway.'

'What, too small?'

'No, too big,' I said.

'Ah yes, the one that got away, huh?' Tom laughed. 'All that way for an adventure that never was. Oh well, better luck next time, hey boys?'

I nodded and shrugged my shoulders. From behind me, I heard Barney chuckle as I said, 'Yeah, better luck next time, I guess.'